THIS WALKER BOOK BELONGS TO:

_____

_____

_____

_____

For Sophie
M. W.
For Felix
L. H.

First published 1997 by Walker Books Ltd
87 Vauxhall Walk, London SE11 5HJ

This edition published 1999

2 4 6 8 10 9 7 5 3 1

Text © 1997 Martin Waddell
Illustrations © 1997 Leo Hartas

This book has been typeset in Monotype Garamond.

Printed in Hong Kong

British Library Cataloguing in Publication Data
A catalogue record for this book is available
from the British Library.

ISBN 0-7445-7213-4

# Mimi's
# Christmas

## MARTIN WADDELL

### illustrated by
### LEO HARTAS

WALKER BOOKS
AND SUBSIDIARIES

LONDON • BOSTON • SYDNEY

Mimi lived with her mouse sisters and brothers beneath the big tree.

"Santa Mouse will come soon," Mimi told her mouse sisters and brothers, as they huddled up close to the fire. "You must write your Santa Mouse notes, so he will know what to put in your stockings."

The mouse brothers and sisters started
scribbling their Santa Mouse notes.

They scribbled ...

and they scribbled ...

and they scribbled ...

and they scribbled …

and they scribbled.

"I can't write Santa's note by myself, I'm too small!" Hugo told Mimi.

"I'll do it for you," said Mimi. "Tell me what to write."

This is the note Mimi wrote.

Dear Santa Mouse,
I hope you are well.
I'd like a BIG drum.
Love from
Hugo Mouse
X
P.S. I'm the small one.

"Does Santa Mouse have drums?" asked Hugo, when they were hanging the lights on their very own mouse Christmas tree.

"Well, he might have a small one," said Mimi. "It has to fit in your stocking."

"A small drum that makes a big BOOM when you bang it?" said Hugo.

"Just wait and see, Hugo," said Mimi.

Christmas Eve came and it snowed.
The mice tumbled and jumbled about
in the snow.

They tumbled ...

and they jumbled ...

and they tumbled …

and they jumbled …

till they all looked like little white mice!

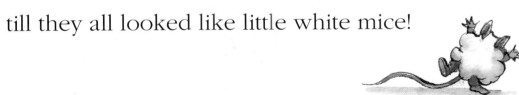

"Supper!" called Mimi, and her mouse sisters and brothers came in from the snow. They had a Christmas Eve feast, huddled close to the fire with mouse lemonade and mouse cake.

"Let's leave Santa Mouse some," Mimi said, and she put mouse cake and mouse lemonade out for Santa, under the mouse Christmas tree in her garden.

"Time for bed, sleepyhead!" Mimi said.
Hugo hung up his mouse stocking at the
end of his little mouse bed. It was a very big
stocking, though he was a very small mouse.
"Is it big enough for my drum?"
Hugo asked.
"Just wait and see, Hugo,"
said Mimi.

The mouse sisters and brothers dreamed of the toys Santa Mouse would bring for their mouse stockings.

They dreamed …

and they dreamed …

and they dreamed …

and they dreamed …

and they dreamed.

All of them dreamed except Hugo.
Hugo was such a small mouse that he
felt too excited to sleep. He got out of
bed and he looked, but there wasn't a
drum in his stocking.

Hugo went looking for Mimi.
"I can't get to sleep and that means
Santa Mouse won't come," Hugo told
Mimi, and he started to cry. "There
won't be a drum in my stocking!"

Mimi took Hugo out to the garden.
"Santa Mouse always comes," Mimi said.
"He comes when our mouse world's asleep.
That's how Santa Mouse works."

Mimi put Hugo to bed. And the next morning…

BOOM! BOOM! BOOM!
"Hugo's got his drum," Mimi's mouse sisters and brothers told Mimi. And …

Christmas was noisy at Mimi's!

# MORE WALKER PAPERBACKS
## For You to Enjoy

### THE CHRISTMAS KITTEN
by Vivian French/Chris Fisher

It's the day before Christmas. Out in the snow, the little black kitten is cold and hungry and lonely. Nobody seems to want him. But, at last, he stumbles on Father Christmas, who knows just where the little kitten belongs!

0-7445-7214-2    £4.99

### THE GOOD LITTLE CHRISTMAS TREE
by Ursula Moray Williams/Gillian Tyler

First published in 1943, this is the classic tale of a heroic little Christmas tree's quest to make himself more beautiful for the poor family that owns him.

"Has a timeless quality that makes it as relevant today as when it was first published… Exquisite illustrations encapsulate the overwhelming beauty and goodness of this uplifting story." *Junior Education*

0-7445-7255-X    £4.99

### RUBY THE CHRISTMAS DONKEY
by Mirabel Cecil/Christina Gascoigne

Poor Ruby is growing old and can't keep herself warm in the winter. So the other animals make her a special gift – a colourful Christmas coat – in this heartwarming seasonal tale.

"Christina Gascoigne's illustrations are a real delight."
*The Sunday Telegraph*

0-7445-6385-2    £4.99

**Walker Paperbacks are available from most booksellers, or by post from B.B.C.S., P.O. Box 941, Hull, North Humberside HU1 3YQ**
**24 hour telephone credit card line 01482 224626**

To order, send: Title, author, ISBN number and price for each book ordered, your full name and address, cheque or postal order payable to BBCS for the total amount and allow the following for postage and packing:
UK and BFPO: £1.00 for the first book, and 50p for each additional book to a maximum of £3.50.
Overseas and Eire: £2.00 for the first book, £1.00 for the second and 50p for each additional book.

Prices and availability are subject to change without notice.